Daddy Frog and the Moon

Pippa Goodhart

Augusta Kirkwood

Frog leapt lily pads without
a worry in the world.

Then a teeny tadpole wriggled out of an egg and said …

This book belongs to

· ·

For all loving but busy daddies – PG

For my wonderful parents, who are always there even when we are apart – AK

Thanks to Pippa and Augusta for taking this leap with us and creating such a wonderful book – LDB

Published by Little Door Books 2019
This edition published 2019

ISBN: 978-1-9999556-2-5

Text copyright © Pippa Goodhart 2019
Illustrations copyright © Augusta Kirkwood 2019

A CIP catalogue record for this book is available from the British Library.

mail@littledoorbooks.co.uk | www.littledoorbooks.co.uk | twitter: @littledoorbooks

"You are my Daddy Frog!
I love you!"

"I love you too,"
said Daddy Frog.

But saying that didn't
seem enough to tell Baby
Frog all that he felt.

"Daddy Frog, Daddy Frog, will you show
me how to squiggle?" said Baby Frog.
"Not now," said Daddy Frog, "because I
want to find you something that will show
you how I love you."

Daddy Frog dived,
plop-splash!
into the pond,
and he swam away.

So Baby Frog squiggled all on her own.

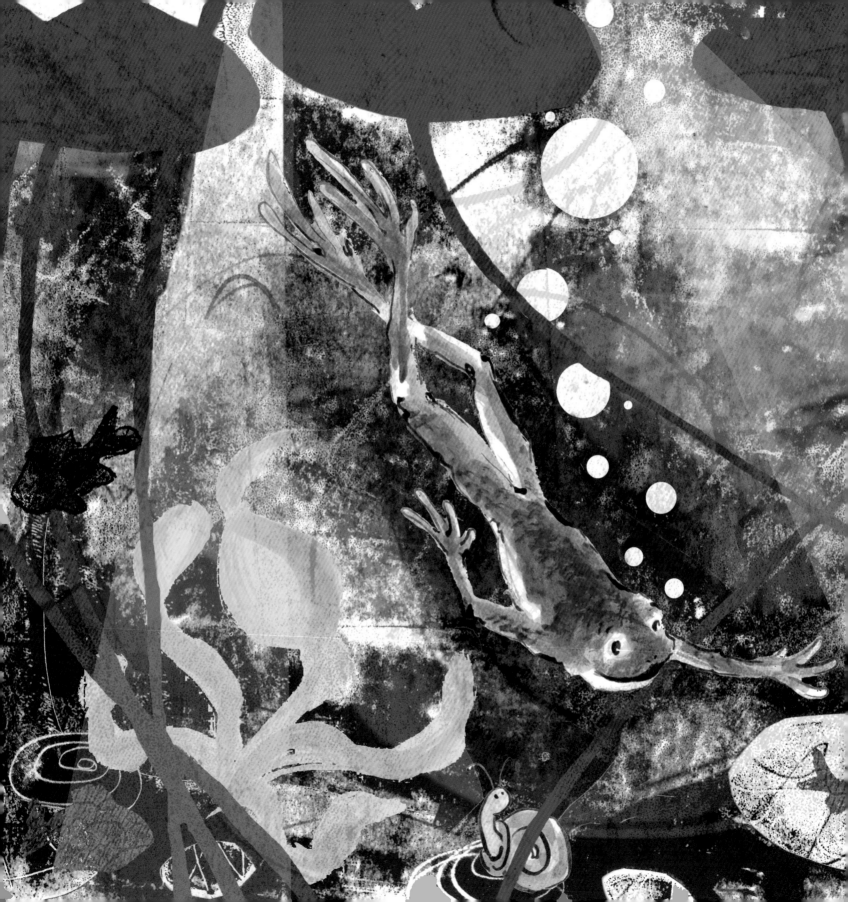

Deep down in the pond Daddy Frog swam, searching until he found a stone that was perfectly round.

"As perfect as my love for Baby Frog," thought Daddy Frog.

"Daddy Frog, you're back!"
said Baby Frog.
"This stone is for you,"
said Daddy Frog.

"Thank you," said Baby Frog.
"But Daddy Frog, Daddy Frog, will
you show me how to swim?"

"Oh, dear," said Daddy Frog.
"The stone is dull out of the water. I must
find something better to show you my love."
And Hop!, off he went again.

So Baby Frog swam all on her own.

Daddy Frog hopped and he searched for days until he found a lovely white lily flower.

"You're back, Daddy Frog!" said Baby Frog.
"This lily is for you," said Daddy Frog.
"Thank you," said Baby Frog, "But Daddy Frog,
Daddy Frog, please will you show me how to hop?"
"Oh, dear," said Daddy Frog. "The lily is wilting.
I must find something better to show you my love."

So Baby Frog tried to hop all by herself.

But it was hard.

Daddy Frog looked up.
He saw the moon
looking marvellous.

"I will give my Baby Frog the moon,"
he decided, and he leapt
as high as the sky!

But, however high Daddy
Frog leapt, he could not
reach the moon.

And soon the moon disappeared behind a cloud.

"Oh dear," sighed Daddy Frog.

But then he heard something happy …

"… Yaaay!" sang Baby Frog. "Daddy Frog, you **DID** help me to hop!"

"Did I?" said Daddy Frog.

"Yes!" said Baby Frog. "I hopped so high it was a leap! Daddy Frog, Daddy Frog, will you leap with me now?"

And Daddy Frog suddenly knew just what to do to show Baby Frog how very much he loved her, and he said …

… "Yes, I would love to!"
So Daddy Frog and Baby
Frog leapt together.

LEAP LEAP LEAP

… until they were both tired.
"Look at the moon, Baby Frog," said Daddy Frog.
"It changes how it looks, but it is always there.
Just like my love for you, Baby Frog,
just like my love for you."

"I knew that, Daddy Frog," said Baby Frog.